Text by John Peel

Cover Illustration by Paul Vaccarello

Interior Illustration by John Nez

Western Publishing Company, Inc.
New York, N.Y.

Your Briefing

Congratulations, you've been hired as a rookie detective for the Acme Detective Agency. Your goal is to outsmart Carmen Sandiego and her gang by solving the cases in this book. Each time you solve a case and make the least amount of moves you'll get a promotion.

There are four cases to solve in this book. To solve each case, start by removing the cards from the insert in the middle of this book. Divide the cards into four groups. You should have the following:

4 Bookmark / Scorecards
4 Stolen Object Cards
8 Suspect Cards
8 Map Cards

Use a different **scorecard** for each game to write down clues and eliminate suspects. When you arrive in a new town use the same card as a **bookmark** to mark the place that you're in while you're investigating—sometimes you'll have to retrace your steps.

Each case involves a stolen object. Decide which case you are going to solve by picking a **stolen object card**. Put the other stolen object cards away until you are ready to solve those cases.

As you read each case you will be given clues about different suspects. Use those clues and the ones on the back of the **suspect cards** to decide which suspect you must capture. When you have made your decision, put the other suspect cards aside. The suspect card you have chosen serves as your warrant for their arrest.

Use the **map cards** for information on the various countries that you'll have to visit while tracking down a suspect. Put aside any cards that don't fit the clues you are given, until you have only one map card left.

Each time you are told to go to a different number in the story, mark that move point on your scorecard. At the end of each game, add up the total points. Check your score on the last page to see if you've earned a promotion.

Now put on your raincoat, make sure you've got a pen or pencil, and get ready to start your first Acme Detective Agency case.

It's been a while since you've had time to relax, but tonight's the night — no work, just play. It's one of those warm, pleasant San Francisco evenings so you decide to walk home. (*Besides, your car is in pretty bad shape — you wish you could afford a new one.*) On the way, you stop and buy a hot dog. Then you decide to live dangerously — and order extra mustard! You stroll toward your favorite movie theater. There's a new detective film that you've been dying to see, and it feels good to be able to just enjoy yourself.

It's a feeling that doesn't last long, however. With a screech of tires and the smell of burning rubber, a car slams to a halt nearby. Suddenly you relax, it's just your secretary.

"What's wrong?" you ask her. "Can't sleep at the office anymore?"

"Funny," she snaps back. "Get in the car. The Chief wants to see you, on-the-double."

You eye the car with a trace of fear. "You driving?" you ask her.

"I wouldn't let you drive," she answers. "You've managed to crash three cars this year!"

"All in the line of duty," you explain. With a sigh, you climb in. Finally, she screeches to a halt in the Acme Detective Agency garage. You're so grateful to arrive in one piece, you feel like kissing the ground.

"Some hot-shot you are," she sneers. "I thought you were supposed to be brave? You had your eyes closed all the way."

"I was watching my life flash before me," you reply, climbing out of the car. "At least, I think it was my life."

You go inside and find the Chief in his office. He's sitting there frowning at the papers on his desk. You've seen this expression before.

"Carmen Sandiego?" you guess.

"Right," he agrees. "Some of her gang have struck again. In Europe, this time. The European police agency Interpol wants our help. You're the only person who has ever outsmarted Carmen, so you're on the case, I'm afraid."

So much for a nice quiet evening, you think to yourself.

He tosses you four files. "Inside each folder are details of the stolen treasures and maps of the countries involved." Then he hands you four separate cards.

"Four objects have been stolen," he says. Pick the case you want to investigate first and then read the card in the file.

"Each time you go somewhere, mark down

your travel points on these cards. You're in line for a promotion, and we'll be using them to grade you when the case is over."

A promotion! Maybe you'll be able to afford a new car or even a trip to Disney World! Better make certain that you keep those travel points carefully noted.

Finally the Chief hands you another batch of cards. "These are snapshots of the members of Carmen's gang. Don't forget to get a warrant for the *right* person before you make an arrest, otherwise the thief will get away."

Now read those files and go where you're told. Good luck."

You take a taxi to the airport, so you have plenty of time to check out the files and determine your first stop.

If you've chosen to recapture:
- *The Parthenon — go to 35*
- *The Little Mermaid — go to 110*
- *The Original copy of "Auld Lang Syne" By Robert Burns — go to 57*
- *Johann Sabastian Bach's Pipe organ — go to 156*

1. Your plane touches down in the city of Bern, Switzerland. Switzerland has not been involved in a foreign war since 1515 A.D. Since 1815 A.D. Switzerland has remained strictly neutral in all wars. For this reason, many international agencies have their headquarters here. Switzerland is also a major banking center, which might explain why Carmen's gang is so interested in the country.

You're met by the local Interpol agent when you get off the plane. He greets you and hands you a list.

"I've done some checking. There are three people who've seen the man you're after and three possible flights he could have taken out of the country."

If you want to stay in Switzerland
and talk to:
The watchmaker — go to 49
The yodeler — go to 155
The banker — go to 119

If you're ready to move on to:
Athens, Greece — go to 74
Sofia, Bulgaria — go to 103
Tirana, Albania — go to 25

2. You've arrived in Edinburgh, Scotland but the only person you see at your meeting place is a puzzled-looking local agent. You ask about your contact, and he shakes his head.

"Ye're daft," he tells you, in his thick scottish brogue. "Ye shouldna be here. Get along to 60 right away."

3. Thera is a small C-shaped island off the Greek coast. About 1500 B.C., a volcano exploded on the island, sinking a part of it and destroying the civilization on nearby Crete. It was this explosion that may have started the legend about the lost continent of Atlantis. But now, Thera is just a sleepy little island. It's not hard to find Hera (who is named after the sister of the Greek mythological god Zeus.)

"*Here-a I am*," she calls with a laugh. You ask her about the woman you're after, and she stops to think.

"I saw her-a, but she didn't stay long. She said she was going to a place that had plenty of olives, and shoes."

You thank her (um, *Hera*) for the help and head back to Athens, Greece (35) to check out this clue.

4. You've come over the sea to Skye — the island of Skye, in Scotland, that is — looking for Gene Yuss. But you're on the wrong track. Go to 99 immediately.

5. You've gone to the Left Bank of the Seine, in Paris. This famous riverside walk is a traditional place for artists to sell their wares to tourists. You spot the artist and ask him about the man you're following.

"But of course I recall him. He wanted me to paint his portrait, but he said he didn't like my style. I told him he didn't know good art when he saw it, and he replied that he was going after machinery next." He smiles at you. "But you — you look like you have good taste. Would you perhaps like me to paint your portrait?"

You tell him some other time, and head back to the airport (123) to check on this new clue.

6. Valencia, the third largest city in Spain, is surrounded by many orchards. You find the fruit inspector you're looking for in a beautiful orange grove. You walk through the grove to talk to him.

"Yes, I remember the man you're after," he tells you. "He had red hair and could hardly speak Spanish. He said he was happy to be going some-

10

where next where they spoke English."

Wishing your own Spanish was better, you thank him kindly for his help and head back to Madrid (160).

7. The Black Forest is a beautiful area of Germany, where the rivers and the trees create a restful and cheery background. This area produces some of the finest children's toys in the world. The toy maker is working on a puppet that looks almost alive. It's kind of creepy. The toy maker stops her work when you ask her about the woman you're after.

"Yes, I recall her," she says, finally. "She was disappointed with the trees and said she was going next to a place where there was fruit on the trees."

Thanking her for her help, you hurry back to Berlin (39).

8. You arrive in Bern, the capital of Switzerland. It's a busy town, but there's no one here to meet you. After a while, you call the local Interpol office. They tell you to go immediately to 60.

9. You're in Paris, which is known as the City of Lights. At night, the whole city comes alive with light. There's no one here to meet you and right now,

you're not feeling very bright. Better get to 60.

10. Ah, Vienna, Austria! The home of the waltz; a dance whose music was made famous by composers from the Strauss family. Vienna's palaces and gardens by the Danube River are world-famous, and you only hope you can get to see them. But it's business first, and you greet the local Interpol agent. She smiles back warmly and hands you a list.

If you want to stay in Vienna and interview:
The innkeeper in Innsbruck — go to 50
Viennese "Fingers" — go to 18
Waltzing Matilde — go to 140

If you're ready to leave for:
San Marino City, San Marino — go to 79
Dublin, Ireland — go to 116
Bucharest, Romania — go to 30

11. Bern is high in the Swiss mountains, and you feel a little giddy at this altitude. Actually, you're feeling giddy because you're in the wrong place. Better head to 60 right away!

12. You arrive in Zagreb, in northern Yugoslavia, and find the shoemaker you're after. The country exports a great deal of its shoes all over Europe.

Yugoslavia has a tradition of fine leather workmanship stretching back hundreds of years.

The old man nods politely to you, and you ask if he's seen the woman you're following.

"Yes," he tells you. "She bought a new pair of shoes from me. Then she asked for directions to the nearest bookstore. She mentioned that she needed a book to help her learn Greek."

Thanking him, you return to Belgrade, (154) to check out this clue.

13. It's not hard to find Patrick the Piper — you can hear the wail of his bagpipes in the distance. He's marching up and down in his garden, playing loudly as you arrive. You try to talk to him, but it's impossible to yell louder than his piping. He finally stops, and you can talk.

"It keeps the birds away from my plants," he tells you.

"And visitors away from the door, probably," you reply. You ask if he's seen the man you're after.

"Aye, that I have," he answers. "A man with no ear for music. He hated my piping. When I told him to clear off, he said he was going to a country where they spoke French."

You thank him and dash back to Kilmarnock,

13

Scotland (57) as fast as you can. You've got to brush up on your own French — mostly, you just want to be well out of range when Patrick starts his piping again!

14. You've arrived in Berlin, the capital of the reunited Germanys. They may have it together, but you don't. You're in the wrong place, so you'd better head for 60 right away.

15. Austria is famous for furniture that is crafted from native timber. You arrive at the small factory, which produces some delightful, hand-carved cabinets, and talk to the head carpenter.

"Yes, I saw the woman you are seeking," he tells you. "She wanted a bedroom set, but couldn't make up her mind which one. She had to leave to catch a plane."

"Any idea where to?" you ask.

"All I know is that she also mentioned something about uranium."

You head back to Vienna (125) to check out this information.

16. You've arrived in Warsaw, Poland. The city was almost destroyed during World War II, but it was rebuilt and is now bustling with life. The local Interpol agent arrives and greets you.

"I've done some checking," she tells you. "And I've managed to gather a list of people who saw the thief you're chasing — and a few places she might have gone."

If you want to stay in Poland and talk to:
The Solidarity member — go to 24
Max from Bialystok — go to 130
The coal miner — go to 118

If you're ready to move on to:
Belgrade, Yugoslavia — go to 36
Edinburgh, Scotland — go to 142
Lisbon, Portugal— go to 81

17. You've tracked Gypsy Rose Lasagna to a small cafe on the outskirts of Sofia, Bulgaria. But here the trail is as cold as yesterday's soup. With a sigh, you head for 99.

18. You find Viennese "Fingers" in the local jail. The police captain tells you that "Fingers" is a pickpocket who was picked up that morning. He has refused to talk until he gets a lawyer. You try your best, but he won't talk to you either. Having no luck here, you head back to Vienna (10) to try again.

15

19. You're now in Edinburgh, the capital of Scotland, but there's no one here to meet you. Puzzled, you ask at the local police station. They hand you a message from the Chief. You read it:

Go straight to 60.

20. Danish bacon is exported all over Europe, along with other Danish foods such as cookies and cheese. The man you want to speak to is a packer in the Danish Bacon Company. As he prepares huge sides of pigs to be shipped to England, you ask about the woman you're trailing.

"I saw her," he tells you. "She bought some bacon from me. She said she was going to get some corn to go with it for her dinner tonight."

You thank him and hurry back to 110 check your clues.

21. Vienna, Austria, home of the waltz! Just the place to dance the night away. And you might as well do that, since there's no one here to meet you. Or, you could just go to 60 right now.

22. Music is a very important part of life in Ireland, and you find you've arrived at a local bar on fiddling night. All the musicians from the area arrive with their violins, ready to com-

pete against one another in bowing up jigs and reels. One of the musicians, however, arrives not with a violin, but with a pipe organ. And a very famous one, at that!

You grab the man, and whisk off his disguise. It's Oly O'Leahy!

"The jig's up," you tell him. When he tries to escape, the fiddlers pick him up and hold him while you check out the stolen Bach pipe organ. It's still in fine shape.

"You picked the wrong place to try and play this," you tell Oly.

"Why?" he asks with a pout. "They said there was a music contest here tonight.

"It's a violin contest, you idiot." The local police arrive to haul him off to jail and to return the stolen pipe organ. Meanwhile, you call the Chief to report your success.

"Well done," he tells you. "Now head straight to the scoring chart at the back of the book to see if you've earned a promotion."

23. You've tracked Ken Hartley Reed to a sleepy little vineyard. Unfortunately, there's no one here at all. Realizing that you've been misled, you pack up and head for 99.

24. You find the Solidarity member at his job

in the metalworking factory. Solidarity, a union founded in 1980, led Poland in its recent break from the ruling Communist Party. The union is very popular in the country. The worker smiles at you, and you ask about the thief you're tracking.

"Yes, I saw a gray-eyed lady. She said she was looking for a good place to buy textiles."

You thank him and head back to Warsaw (16) to check out these clues.

25. You're in Tirana, Albania, the capital of Albania. This is one of the most controlled countries in the world. The ruling Communist Party has secret police everywhere. You'd almost like to see one of them, because there's no one here to meet you. Finally, you give up and head to 60.

26. San Marino is a tiny country, and postage stamps are one of their main exports. They are constantly issuing new sets of stamps to commemorate events. The person you're looking for is an artist, working on a new set of stamps. You find her in her studio.

"Do you have to paint in all the words?" you joke.

"No," she tells you seriously. "The words are done when my picture is reduced to stamp size."

You admire her artwork. "It's a shame it'll end up so small."

"Yes," she agrees. "But at least it will be seen by a lot of people."

"Speaking of seeing," you ask, "I understand you've seen the thief I'm after."

"He stopped by and tried to steal some stamps," she replies. "He was mailing a lot of letters. I chased him out. Oh, yes, he dropped a book on teaching yourself German."

You wish her luck with her stamps and head back to (79) to check out the clue she gave you.

27. You've reached Berlin, the capital of Germany. There's no one here to meet you — and no messages for you, either. The only thing you can do is go to 60.

28. You arrive on the grounds of a large Scottish castle, wondering what or who is a Ghillie. When you ask at the gate, you're told that he's the head gamekeeper of the land. He's out at the moment, making sure that the deer roaming the estate are in good shape. The gateman gives you directions, and you set off after the Ghillie.

As you enter the woods, someone jumps out of the bushes at you. Thinking quickly, you spin around and do a quick judo flip on him. He sails

19

right into a tree and is knocked out. It's the Ghillie, you discover, but he's also secretly in the pay of Carmen's gang. Obviously, you're getting very close to the thief, and the Ghillie was trying to stop you. Time to head back to Edinburgh (142) and follow another lead!

29. You've arrived in the coastal city of Varna, Yogoslavia. You followed the trail of Oly O'Leahy to the docks, only to learn that Oly left months ago on a boat to South America. Obviously, this is a dead-end trail. Go straight to 99.

30. You're in Bucharest, Romania, but you may as well be in bed, taking a rest. There's no one here for you. Time to head to 60.

31. This is Madrid, capital of Spain. It's a busy city, but you don't see anyone waiting for you. When you ask at the office for messages, you're handed a fax from the Chief: Go to 60.

32. Albania is a very poor country that needs many items that aren't made within its borders. Traders often travel down the coast to Greece to get things. Then they travel back to Albania with their cargo, to sell for lots of money. Your contact is one of these traders. You mention the woman you're after.

"I saw her," he tells you. "But it'll cost you."

You pay the trader, and he smiles. "This woman you seek left here, and she went to a country where she could buy some good wine."

You leave the trader to his work and head back to Tirana(52) to check out the clue.

33. You find the schoolteacher dismissing her class, and when she's free, you ask about the man you're trailing.

"Yes, he was here," she tells you. "He wanted me to teach him to speak Turkish. When I told him it would take about a year, he said he couldn't spare the time and left."

"Any other clues?" Did he say exactly where he was going?" you ask.

"Sorry, detective, but not a word."

Thanking her, you head back to Belgrade, Yugoslavia (131) to consider her clue.

34. Hannover, Germany is an old town, much of which was destroyed during World War II. Hannover has since been rebuilt with plenty of parks, earning it the name of "the garden city."

Hans, the man you're looking for, is a gardener in one of the most famous parks, called the Stadtpark. When you find him, he's tending his plants carefully. You ask about the man you're after.

"Ach, he was here," Hans tells you. "He was trampling on my flowers, so I took him by the scruff of his stupid neck and threw him out. I noticed that he had brown eyes. He kept muttering something about dancing. I think he said he wanted to go waltzing. What a lunatic!"

You thank Hans and wish him well with his plants. Then you head back to Leipzig (156).

35. At one time, Athens, Greece was one of the world's most beautiful cities, with many ancient buildings and ruins. But now the pollution from passing cars is threatening to crumble away all those treasures unless something can

be done to protect them. You wish you could help, but that's not your job right now. You've got to get the Parthenon back where it belongs.

You talk to the local Inspector of Police, who has done some preliminary work for you. He hands you a list of people who saw the thief and a list of possible places where the crook might have gone.

If you want to stay in Greece and investigate:
The olive merchant — *go to 109*
The university professor — *go to 157*
Hera from Thera — *go to 3*

If you think that the thief has gone to:
Belgrade, Yugoslavia — *go to 59*
Madrid, Spain — *go to 133*
Berlin, Germany — *go to 27*

36. You've arrived in Belgrade, the capital of Yugoslavia. There's no one here to meet you, and after a while, you call the local Interpol office. They tell you to hurry to 60.

37. Monasteries are still dotted all over Greece, with many of them located on mountains. Thankfully, Emmanuel, the monk you are looking for, is in a monastery that's easy to reach. You ask for him at the door. The monk nods and calls out: "O come, o come, Emmanuel!"

Emmanuel is a young man, bright and cheery. You ask about the man you're looking for.

"I saw him when I was in the orchard," Emmanuel tells you.

"He has brown hair, and he stopped to ask me for directions. He said he was looking for a good place to buy corn."

You thank Emmanuel for his help and hurry back to Athens (74).

38. The gypsy violinist that you're seeking plays in a popular restaurant in the town of Oradea. You arrive as he's playing, and you stop to listen. You're surprised at how good he is. You want to dance as he plays. When he's done, you congratulate him and then ask about the man you're after.

"He was here for dinner," the violinist replies. "As he was leaving, he mentioned something about going to a good place for fruit."

You give him a nice tip and tell him you loved his music. Then you head back to Bucharest, Romania (91) to follow up on this new lead.

39. Your plane has landed in Berlin, capital of the new Germany. Not so long ago, East Germany and West Germany were two sepa-

rate countries, but now they are one again. You still remember the thrill that went around the world when the Berlin Wall was torn down. But, at the moment, there are other things to think about.

The local Interpol officer greets you. He hands you a sheet of paper that lists people who saw the thief you're tracking and possible places she might have gone.

If you want to stay in Germany
and interview:
The cook — go to 55
The toy maker — go to 7
The factory worker — go to 105

If you're ready to leave for:
Madrid, Spain — go to 31
Belgrade, Yugoslavia — go to 141
Sofia, Bulgaria — go to 88

40. You arrive at a haggis-tasting on the trail of Ken Hartley Reed. You try a little haggis — a popular local dish — but you think it tastes terrible. The word terrible just about describes your luck, too, because Ken isn't here. Head for 99.

41. Your plane lands in Bern, Switzerland but there's no one here to meet you. You ask at the airline desk, and there's a message telling you to go straight to 60.

42. In Ireland they take their music very seriously. You find the harpist you're looking for practicing the lap-sized instrument. He is playing a lively tune known as a planxty. As you applaud, the harpist looks up. He recognizes you immediately. He whips out a small arrow. Using the harp as a bow, he aims the arrow at you.

But you're on your toes. You pick up a chair to use as a shield. After the arrow smacks into it, you toss the chair at the harpist. This knocks him out before he can strike again. He must be a member of Carmen's gang!

As you call the local police, you spot something in the harpist's pocket. You pull it out and discover it's his sheet music. But in the middle of the music is a list containing the addresses of all of Carmen's gang! Now you can arrest the thief!

If you think the thief is:

Ken Hartley Reed — go to 75

Kitty Litter — go to 95

Gypsy Rose Lasagna — go to 124

Russ T. Hinge — go to 63

Minnie Series — go to 152

26

Oly O'Leahy — go to 22
Lynn Gweeny — go to 168
Gene Yuss — go to 112

43. You arrive at a small barbershop in Seville, and the barber smiles as you enter.

"Ah, you come for a little trim?" he asks.

"No, I've come for a little information," you reply. "I've heard that you've seen the thief I'm after."

27

He nods. "That I did. She came to have her blond hair trimmed. Although I speak Spanish, She spoke only German, saying she had to practice. She also said she had to change her money to shillings. You thank him and head back to Madrid (133) to check out the latest clues.

44. The cathedral of Notre Dame stands on an island in the Seine River. Begun in 1163 A.D. and completed in 1313 A.D., Notre Dame is considered one of the masterpieces of Gothic architecture. It is very impressive indeed, and you wish you had time for a tour, but you have to find the lunch room. It's a small building selling snacks, and you ask the old man inside about the thief you're chasing.

"Ah, she stopped here," he tells you. "A black-haired lady, is it not so? I asked her if she liked the building, and she said she preferred to watch ships being built and that that was where she was going next. That woman had no sense of beauty!"

"None at all," you agree as you head back to 61 and check your information.

45. You arrive in the lovely little town of Plovdiv, Bulgaria and ask around for Lynn Gweeny. But nobody has seen her, so you're left with only one choice — to go to 99.

46. You've arrived in Dublin, the capital of Ireland. Dublin was once controlled by England; the Irish Free State came into being in 1921 after a long rebellion. Though there is still much unrest in Northern Ireland (which is still a part of Great Britain), Ireland itself is a peaceful country, renowned for its music, its glassware, and its beautiful countryside.

The local agent arrives. She's a pretty young girl with a ready smile and a delightful accent, and she hands you a very short list.

"'Tis little enough, to be sure," she tells you. "But it should be plenty, I'm thinking."

You examine the list.

If you decide to talk to:

The peat moss cutter — go to 144

Keara from Kinsale — go to 132

The harpist — go to 42

47. Portugal was once conquered by the Moors, a group of people of North African descent. They ruled much of Portugal and Spain from the 8th through the 13th centuries. As you travel through Portugal you can still see many relics of Moorish rule in the country.

Soon you arrive in the town of Silves, which is set high on a hill. At the top of the hill is an old Moorish castle. Suddenly you spot Kitty Litter sizing up the castle — obviously planning her next theft!

You tiptoe up behind her and tap her on the shoulder. She jumps in the air and then spins around.

"Hi, Kitty," you greet her. "Cat got your tongue?"

"I thought I'd lost you, flatfoot," she hisses as she tries to claw you with her long fingernails. But you're prepared. You pull a handful of catnip from your pocket. Smelling the fresh scent, Kitty suddenly smiles and relaxes. She can't resist catnip.

The local police arrive to take Kitty to jail. "Don't forget to ask her to tell you where she's hidden the Parthenon," you remind them. "She's quite a cat-burglar, that one." Then you call the Chief to report your success.

Naturally, he's overjoyed. "There may well be a promotion in this for you," he says. "Why not head for the scoring chart at the back of the book and find out?"

48. You've arrived in Madrid, the capital of Spain. As you get off the plane, a man bumps into you. As he apologizes, he slips you a note. It reads: Go to 60.

49. Switzerland is famous for its wonderful

clocks and watches, as well as the skilled crafts-
men who make them. You stop in front of a clock
store and decide to walk in. The shop is filled with
the sound of ticking. Everywhere you look, there
are clocks — cuckoo clocks, pendulum clocks, wall
clocks, mirror clocks . . . You hope you'll be out of
here before they all strike the hour!

The watchmaker is a cheery old man, and
you ask him about the thief you're after.

"He was in here looking for a new watch," the
old man tells you. "He tried to steal one while
my back was turned! But I was too quick for him
and chased him out. He ran so fast, he dropped
a book on learning Greek."

You thank him and head back to 1 to check
on this clue. All at once the clocks begin to
chime, just as you close the door. . .

50. Innsbruck, Austria is a town set on the
banks of the river Inn, high in the Tirol
Mountains. Here, old, pretty houses crowd long,
narrow streets. You thread your way through
them to the inn you're looking for, which is on
the Herzog-Friedrich-Strasse, a main street
dating from the fifteenth century. Once inside,
you find the innkeeper.

"Yes," he tells you when you ask about the
thief, "the man you're looking for stopped in

here. This is the best route over the mountains, you see, and he mentioned he was on his way to buy some special postage stamps."

You thank him for his help and head back to Vienna (10) to check out this clue.

51. You've arrived in Lisbon, the capital of Portugal. Back in the fourteenth century, Portugal was famous for its explorers, the most famous one being Prince Henry the Navigator.

Prince Henry was also famous for establishing schools for sailors who hoped to go out and discover new countries.

You hope to discover an old crook.

The local Interpol agent greets you. "Not much to go on, I'm afraid," he tells you, handing over a short list. You examine it.

If you want to interview:
The bullfighter — go to 72
The fisherman — go to 161
The dancer — go to 129

52. The plane lands you in Tirana, Albania, the capital of Albania. It's a poor country, ruled by a national Communist Party. Albania is not a very well-known country, since it keeps very much to itself.

You discover that one of the local police officials is waiting for you.

"There's not much I can do for you," he explains. "But I have managed to find a few witnesses for you and a few places where your crook may have gone. Good luck in your search."

You figure you'll need it, and you look over the list.

If you want to stay in Albania and talk to:
The smuggler — go to 32
The factory worker — go to 166
The farmer — go to 114

If you're ready to depart for:
Paris, France — go to 61
Bern, Switzerland — go to 8
Lisbon, Portugal — go to 85

53. So this is Sofia, capital of Bulgaria. Sofia means "wisdom," and you've shown plenty to have gotten this far. Now you're greeted by the local police captain, who smartly salutes you and hands you a small slip of paper.

"There are three people who may be able to tell you where your thief is," the captain explains. You examine the piece of paper.

If you want to investigate:
The farmer from Varna — go to 107

The tour guide — go to 151
The fisherman — go to 135

54. The castle of Rocca Guaita, in the tiny country of San Marino, stands on one of the three peaks of Mount Titano, overlooking San Marino City. It's a steep climb, but you arrive at the castle gate and ask for the guard you want to speak to. After a moment, he arrives and greets you. You ask him about the man you're after.

"Yes, I saw him. He was here for a while. We chatted a bit, and he told me that he was interested in wheat."

You thank the guard and head back to town (79) to investigate further.

55. Germany has many famous foods, and the cooks in the best restaurants are kept very busy. The cook you're looking for is dashing around, preparing for the restaurant's opening. He manages to take a short break to answer your questions.

"Yes, I saw the woman you're after. She wanted to know the recipe for my famous Black Forest Cake. When I refused to tell her, she left in a bad mood, mumbling something about bauxite and coal."

"Did you notice anything about the way she

looked?" you ask.

The cook thinks for a moment. "All that I remember is that she had brown eyes." You thank him and head back to 39 to check on these clues.

56. You've arrived at a porridge factory. Scots like to eat plenty of oatmeal (which they call porridge), often with a little salt added. It doesn't sounds too tasty to you. Obviously Gypsy Rose Lasagnafeels the same way, because she's nowhere to be found. With a sigh, you head for 99.

57. You've arrived in Kilmarnock, Scotland, home of Robert Burns, the man who wrote the famous song "Auld Lang Syne."

You're met by a Chief Inspector from Scotland Yard, who takes you to the exact scene of the crime.

"Ah, it's breaking our hearts," he tells you. "Burns is the finest poet Scotland ever knew, and this song is one of the best known in the world. This theft is a bad case."

"Burns us all up," you agree. "What do we have to go on?"

"Just a few clues and some possible places that the thief may have fled." The Chief Inspector hands you a list.

If you want to stay in Scotland and investigate:
Patrick the Piper — go to 13
The Loch Ness punster — go to 159
Heather from the Hebrides — go to 94

If you think the crook has gone to:
Paris, France — go to 123
Belgrade, Yugoslavia — go to 82
Bern, Switzerland — go to 41

58. In the hills of Germany, there are shepherds who guard their flocks of sheep with the aid of dogs. In Europe, these intelligent and strong dogs are called Alsatians, but in the United States, they're better known as German shepherds.

You're relieved to discover that it's the dog's owner who has the clue you're after, and not the dog. Though it seems friendly, it's awfully large and has very big teeth.

"Yes, I saw the man you're after," he tells you. "He had brown eyes and was scaring my sheep, so I told him to clear off. He laughed and said he was going to a steel works."

Hmmm . . . He'd probably find plenty to steal there! After you thank the shepherd and stroke his dog, you head back to Leipzig, Germany (156) to check out your clues.

59. You've reached Belgrade, the capital of Yugoslavia. While you're waiting at the airport, you hear your name being paged. You pick up the phone, and it's the Chief.

"What are you doing there?" he growls. "You should be at 60."

"I'm almost there," you tell him.

"Well, go there now!" he yells. You head right out.

60. It seems as though you've been misled by Carmen's gang. You'd better return to the last place you had clues (you did remember to mark your place, didn't you?) and check out your destination again. Don't forget to add the travel points.

61. You're in Paris, the famous city of sights and delights, tiny sidewalk cafes, the Eiffel Tower, and the Louvre Museum — so much to see and do. But, sadly, you're here to work, not to sightsee. The local lady from Interpol arrives and greets you.

"We've discovered three people who saw the thief you're after, and three places where she may have gone." She hands you a slip of paper.

If you want to stay in Paris and look into:

The lunch room of Notre Dame — go to 44
The Eiffel Tower flower girl — go to 73
Madeline the orphan — go to 106

If you're ready to depart for:
Berlin, Germany — go to 150
Warsaw, Poland — go to 16
Edinburgh, Scotland — go to 97

62. Running through the center of Paris, the Seine is a river that sees much life and beauty. Tours are very popular, and there are many boat trips that leave from various spots along the riverbank. You find the boatman that you seek and him ask about the man you're after.

"That man was a madman!" the boatman exclaims. "I was taking a group of tourists on a trip when he tried to sneak aboard without paying. I was so furious, I threw him right into the river. He must have been crazy!"

"In-Seine," you tell the boatman. "Can you tell me anything else?"

"Only that he dropped a book on potato-growing when I tossed him out of my boat."

You thank the man and head back to your base (123) to check out this new clue.

63. You've trailed Russ T. Hinge into the countryside by Galway Bay, Ireland. As you look around, you see rolling green hills and tiny cottages with thatched roofs. What you don't see is any sign of Hinge, and you head for 99.

64. Foma has a small farm near Sozopol, Bulgaria, on the coast of the Black Sea. You arrive there as he's harvesting wheat, one of the biggest export items in Bulgaria. Foma takes a short break from his work to answer your questions.

"Yes, I saw the woman you're after. She stopped by here on her way west. She mentioned that she was heading off to do some fishing."

You thank Foma and head back to Sofia (88) to check out your new clue.

65. You arrive at the Amalienborg Palace. The Danish Royal family has lived here since the eighteenth century. You find Poul just getting off duty. You ask him about the thief you're hunting.

"She was here," he tells you. "I thought she was acting oddly, so I told her to leave. As she walked by, I saw she was carrying a book on corn."

You thank Poul and head back to base (110) to check on this clue.

66. Your plane lands in Madrid, the capital of sunny Spain. But there's no Interpol agent here. You call the local office, and the puzzled receptionist tells you that you should be at 60.

67. Spanish oranges are considered very tasty and are sent all over the world. You arrive in the Spanish orchards to find the young woman you're looking for.

She's carefully checking the oranges, making certain that they are ready to be picked. You ask her about the man you're looking for.

"I remember him," she tells you. "Red-headed. He told me he's not fond of orange juice. He said he liked milk better and was going to a place that made lots of dairy products."

You thank her and head back to Madrid (160) to consider these clues.

68. Vienna is considered to be the home of psychiatry, since Sigmund Freud did his most important work here. There are still many psychiatrists who carry on in Freud's tradition. You find the psychiatrist you're looking for. You ask him about the woman you're hunting. He looks at you with a kindly expression.

"How long have you had this urge to follow people all over the world?" he asks you, getting out his notebook.

"Ever since I became a detective. Look, let me ask the questions. You just answer them."

"Ah! Classic hostility behavior. I am used to this. Wouldn't you feel more comfortable on the couch?"

"I'm not a patient," you tell him. "But I am losing my patience!"

"You are obviously under great stress," he says, smiling. "Perhaps you need to rest."

"What I need are some answers," you tell him. Since you're obviously getting nowhere here, you get up to leave.

"Perhaps we'll do better next time," he tells you. "If you continue your visits I think we'll have you cured in ten or twelve years."

"I'm not the one who's batty," you reply. With a deep sigh, you head back to 125 to find a better lead to follow.

69. The vineyard is a small place nestled in a little hillside. There the wine maker is hard at work in a small factory. You look around and see that grapes are put into a big rotating metal barrel.

"Why aren't you stomping the grapes with your feet?" you ask.

"Oh we don't do that anymore," says the wine

maker. "Modern machinery is much more efficient. And it's nice not having to go to bed with purple feet every night!"

The grapes are pressed in the barrels and then stored in metal tanks where they slowly turn into wine. The wine maker has to make sure that everything's done correctly, or the vineyard will end up with undrinkable wine. But he kindly stops after awhile and listens to your questions about the thief you're hunting.

"Yes, she was here. She tried to steal a bottle of our best wine, but I saw her, and she rushed out quickly. In her haste, she dropped a book about fertilizers."

You thank him for his help and wish him well with the wine. Then you head back to Belgrade, Yugoslavia (154) to check your clues.

70. You arrive at Albania on the shores of the Black Sea, looking for Gene Yuss. There's a lot going on, but there's no sign of Yuss anywhere. Eventually, you give up looking and head to 99.

71. You discover that Transylvania, the home of the legendary vampire Count Dracula, is now a part of Romania. You expect Transylvania to be a land full of brooding castles and dark, haunted woods, but instead it's a pleasant and cheerful place.

Sylvie lives in Cluj, the largest city in the region. You ask her about the man you're after.

"I saw him," she says. "He told me he was on his way to look for uranium."

You thank her and head back to Bucharest, (91), glad to have gotten away without meeting any vampires.

72. Portugal, like Spain, is famous for its bull-fighting. But in Portugal, the bulls are not killed in the rings, as they are in Spain. The Portuguese way sounds less cruel to you, but still you wonder if the bullfighters are sane. After all, they face down bulls with just cloaks!

You find the bullfighter you're looking for practicing in the ring when you arrive.

As soon as he sees you, he opens the gate to the bullpen. A huge animal rushes out. When it sees you, it pauses, then charges right at you.

Quickly, you pull off your raincoat and hold it out to one side. The bull hurtles past, dragging the coat on its horn. The coat tears and flies out of your grip. You're just glad it was the coat that was gored, and not you. Before the bull can turn around, you grab the bullfighter and run for safety.

When you catch your breath, you call the police to arrest the man, who is obviously one of Carmen's gang. The police arrive to take him away, and you find that there's a slip of paper hidden in his fancy hat. Pulling out the paper, you shout for joy. You now have the addresses for most of Carmen's gang!

If you think that the thief you're after is:

Kitty Litter — go to 47

Ken Hartley Reed — go to 23

Russ T. Hinge — go to 149

Lynn Gweeny — go to 96

Gypsy Rose Lasagna — go to 165

Gene Yuss — go to121

Oly O'Leahy — go to 80

Minnie Series — go to 137

73. The Eiffel Tower is one of the world's most famous structures. It was built by Alexandre Gustav Eiffel for the 1889 Paris Exhibition. It stands 1,056 feet tall and is a popular tourist attraction. At the base of the tower, you find the

flower girl beside a cart filled with hundreds of fresh flowers. You ask her about the woman you're trailing.

"Oh, her!" she complains. "Ah, she tried to steal some of my flowers, the black-haired wretch! I boxed her ears and sent her packing."

"Do you have any idea where she went?" you ask.

"Well, she had been reading a book about coal mining. It was at the top of the bag she carried. I noticed that a page was marked by airline tickets."

You thank her and hurry back (61) to check out the clues.

74. Your plane lands at the airport in Athens, Greece. Athens was once the seat of learning and culture for the whole world. It contains ruins that are over two thousand years old. Today these ruins are tourist attractions. You wish you had the time to visit some of them, but the hunt for Carmen's gang comes first.

The local Interpol agent arrives and hands you a short list. "I've managed to find you a few people who spotted the thief. There are only three flights he could have taken to leave the country."

If you want to stay in Greece and talk to:

☞

Emmanuel the monk— go to 37
The sailor — go to 98
Zoe and Chloe — go to 16

If you'd ready to leave for:
Paris, France — go to 9
Madrid, Spain — go to 66
Belgrade, Yugoslavia — go to 131

75. You're in Portugal. Sorry, Ken Hartley Reed is hardly here. Head to 99.

76. You arrive in Almagro, a small town in Spain. Here you find Dulcinea, who works as a maid in a hotel. You ask her about the woman you're after, and she thinks for a moment.

"Yes, I saw her. She stayed overnight. She had blonde hair. When she left, she mentioned that she was going to look at a steel manufacturing plant." You thank her and head back to Madrid (133) to note this new information.

77. You've taken the high road, you've taken the low road — but Minnie Series hasn't arrived in Scotland before you. In fact, she's nowhere to be found. Time for you to head to 99.

78. Your plane touches down in Lisbon, the capital of Portugal. No one is waiting to meet you. You call the local office. The secretary tells you to hurry to 60.

79. You drive out of Italy and are now in the republic of San Marino. San Marino is surrounded by Italy, and is one of the world's smallest countries. It's just twenty-four square miles — smaller than most cities in the United States.

You're met by the local Interpol officer, a pretty young lady. She's been busy making a list of people who have seen the robber you're tracking and three places that the thief might have gone. She hands you the list.

If you want to stay in San Marino and interview:

The postage stamp artist — go to 26
The castle guard — go to 54
The farmer — go to 100

If you're ready to move on to:
Edinburgh, Scotland — go to 2
Bern, Switzerland — go to 148
Bucharest, Romania — go to 91

80. You're on the island of Madeira, a Portuguese territory, which is the home of the world-famed

Madeira wine. But that's about all you'll find here, because there's no sign of Oly O'Leahy. You'd better head for 99.

81. You arrive in Lisbon, but there's no one here to meet you. You discover a postcard has been left for you at the airport information desk. On it is a message: Go to 60.

82. Your plane touches down in Belgrade, Yugoslavia and you hurry out to the information desk. There's nobody to meet you, so you call the local office. The secretary is puzzled to hear from you.

"What are you doing here?" she asks. "You should be at 60."

83. Your boat steams into the Copenhagen harbor, but you're still at sea because there's nobody here to meet you. When you call Interpol, they tell you to pack your bags and head straight for 60.

84. Vienna's streets are filled with friendly little cafes and imposing restaurants. The waiter you're looking for works in a small cafe by the side of the Danube River. He brings you a cup of coffee, you ask him about the woman you're trailing.

Lynn Gweeny

Sex: Female
Hair: Black
Eyes: Grey
Favorite Food: Russian
Occupation: Owns the Lot O' Bologna
Weakness: Very clumsy and hot tempered.

Gypsy Rose Lasagna

Sex: Female
Hair: Black
Eyes: Blue
Favorite Food: Tacos
Occupation: Owns a tea room
Weakness: Always trying getting people to eat.

Kitty Litter

Sex: Female
Hair: Blond
Eyes: Hazel
Favorite Food: Kibbles & Bits
Occupation: Owns a pet shop
Weakness: A sucker for stray animals.

Minnie Series

Sex: Female
Hair: Blond
Eyes: Blue
Favorite Food: TV Dinners
Occupation: Star of the soap opera, "As All My Children Turn On Me, I'm Entering General Hospital."
Weakness: Loves to give interviews and pose.

Gypsy Rose Lasagna

Lynn Gweeny

Minnie Series

Kitty Litter

Russ T. Hinge

Oly O' Leahy

Ken Hartley Reed

Gene Yuss

Oly O'Leahy

Sex: Male
Hair: Red
Eyes: Blue
Favorite Food: Freeze dried rations
Occupation: Mountain climber
Weakness: Totally afraid of heights.

Russ T. Hinge

Sex: Male
Hair: Blond
Eyes: Hazel
Favorite Food: Day old Fish n' Chips with mushy peas.
Occupation: Handyman
Weakness: Has a severe allergy and is always sneezing.

Gene Yuss

Sex: Male
Hair: Black
Eyes: Brown
Favorite Food: Nouvelle cuisine — loves to pay big bucks for small portions.
Occupation: Sells dehydrated water and liquid ice to campers.
Weakness: A snob.

Ken Hartley Reed

Sex: Male
Hair: Brown
Eyes: Brown
Favorite Food: World War II C-Rations
Occupation: Hairdresser
Weakness: Cannot finish a single thing.

DENMARK

Capital: Copenhagen
Language: Danish
Currency: Krone
Area: 16,633 square miles
Agriculture: Dairy products
Industry: Machinery, textiles, furniture
Natural Resources: Fish, wood

FEDERAL REPUBLIC OF GERMANY

Capital: Berlin
Language: German
Currency: Mark
Area: 137,787 square miles
Agriculture: Grain, potatoes, sugar beets
Industry: Steel, ships, cars, chemicals
Natural Resources: Coal, potash, lignite, uranium

SCOTLAND

Capital: Edinburgh
Languages: English
Currency: Pounds
Area: 30,412 square miles
Agriculture: Wheat, barley, cattle
Industry: Textiles, ship building, fishing
Natural Resources: Coal, fish

IRELAND

Capital: Dublin
Languages: Gaelic, English
Currency: Pound
Area: 27, 136 square miles
Industry: Textiles, machinery
Agriculture: Meat, dairy products
Natural Resources: Tourism, liquor, fish

SWITZERLAND

Capital: Bern
Area: 15,941 square miles
Language: German, French, Italian
Currency: Franc
Agriculture: Grains, potatoes, beets
Industry: Machinery, tools, watches, chocolate
Natural Resources: Salt

FRANCE

Capital: Paris
Area: 220,668 square miles
Language: French
Currency: Franc
Agriculture: Grains, corn, rice, wine vineyards
Industry: Mining, tourism, wheat
Natural Resources: Bauxite, iron coal

SPAIN

Capital: Madrid
Language: Spanish
Currency: Peseta
Area: 194,896 square miles
Agriculture: Olives, grapes, citrus fruits
Industry: Iron, steel, cars, machinery
Natural Resources: Mercury, uranium, lead

PORTUGAL

Capital: Lisbon
Language: Portuguese
Currency: Escudo
Area: 36,390 square miles
Agriculture: Cork, wood, food, wine
Industry: Clothing, textiles
Natural Resources: Fish, sulfur, iron, tin

ROMANIA

Capital: Bucharest
Area: 91,699 square miles
Language: Romanian, Hungarian, German
Currency: Leu
Agriculture: Corn, wheat, oilseeds
Industry: Steel, metals, machinery
Natural Resources: Oil, gas, coal, wood

BULGARIA

Capital: Sofia
Area: 44,365 square miles
Language: Bulgarian, Turkish, Greek
Currency: Lev
Agriculture: Grains, fruit, corn
Industry: Chemicals, machinery clothing
Natural Resources: Lead, bauxite, coal, oil

POLAND

Capital: Warsaw
Area: 120,727 square miles
Language: Polish
Currency: Zloty
Agriculture: Grains, potatoes, tobacco
Industry: Shipbuilding, chemicals, metals
Natural Resources: Coal, copper, zinc

AUSTRIA

Capital: Vienna
Area: 32,374 square miles
Language: German
Currency: Schilling
Agriculture: Grains, potatoes, beets
Industry: Steel, machinery, glass
Natural Resources: Wood water power

ALBANIA

Capital: Tirana
Area: 11,100 square miles
Language: Albanian, Greek
Currency: Lek
Agriculture: Corn, wheat, cotton
Industry: Chemicals, fertilizer, textiles
Natural Resources: Chromium, coal, oil, wood

GREECE

Capital: Athens
Area: 51,146 square miles
Language: Greek
Currency: Drachma
Agriculture: Grains, corn, olives, raisins, figs
Industry: Textiles, chemicals wine
Natural Resources: Bauxite, lignite, oil

YUGOSLAVIA

Capital: Belgrade
Area: 98,766 square miles
Language: Serbo-Croatian, Macedonian, Slovenian
Currency: Dinar
Agriculture: Corn, grains, tobacco
Industry: Steel, wood products, cement, textiles
Natural Resources: Bauxite, lead

SAN MARINO

Capital: San Marino
Area: 24 square miles
Language: Italian
Currency: Lira
Agriculture: None
Industry: Postage stamps, tourism, woolen products
Natural Resources: None

THE LITTLE MERMAID

Location: Copenhagen, Denmark
Background: The famous storyteller Hans Christian Anderson wrote a tale about a little mermaid who fell in love with a human. To commemorate the writer, artist Edward Ericksen was asked to create a bronze statue of The Little Mermaid. The statue was placed on a rock in Copenhagen Harbor in 1913, and is now one of the best-known sights of the city.

To investigate this crime: Go to 110

THE PARTHENON

Location: Athens, Greece
Background: The Parthenon is the ruined temple of Athena and stands on a hill (Acropolis) above Athens. It was built by Ictinus and Callicrates. Work began on the temple in 477 B.C., with foundations reaching down 40 feet into rock. It was finished in 432 B.C., and originally contained a gold and ivory statue of Athena, goddess of wisdom.

To investigate this crime: Go to 35

JOHANN SEBASTIAN BACH'S PIPE ORGAN

Location: Leipzig, Germany
Background: Johann Sebastian Bach (1685-1750) is one of the greatest composers who ever lived and was considered a master organ builder. His vast output of music included the "The Goldberg Variations,"and the six Brandenberg Concertos, and many religious hymns.

To investigate this crime: Go to 156

ROBERT BURNS' SONG: *Auld Lang Syne*

Location: Kilmarnock, Scotland
Background: Robert Burns (1759-1796) is considered one of Scotland's greatest poets. His main work, *Poems, Chiefly in the Scottish Dialect*, was published in 1786, when he was just 27. Among his verses is the well-known "Auld lang syne," or "Old long since" still sung every New Year's Eve around the world. It was written in 1788. He wrote over 300 songs in all.

To investigate this crime: Go to 57

THE PARTHENON

THE LITTLE MERMAID

ROBERT BURNS' SONG:
Auld Lang Syne

JOHANN SEBASTIAN
BACH'S PIPE ORGAN

SCORE CARD 1

Stolen Object: _____

Clues: _____
_____
_____
_____
_____

**Suspect
to arrest:** _____

Move points

Total Move points: _____

Total Game Score: _____

SCORE CARD 2

Stolen Object: _____

Clues: _____
_____
_____
_____
_____

**Suspect
to arrest:** _____

Move points

Total Move points: _____

Total Game Score: _____

SCORE CARD 3

Stolen Object: _____

Clues: _____
_____
_____
_____
_____

**Suspect
to arrest:** _____

Move points

Total Move points: _____

Total Game Score: _____

SCORE CARD 4

Stolen Object: _____

Clues: _____
_____
_____
_____
_____

**Suspect
to arrest:** _____

Move points

Total Move points: _____

Total Game Score: _____

"She was here," he tells you. "She mentioned that next she was going to a place where she could get lots of baked potatoes."

After you finish your coffee, you head back (125) to check out this new clue.

85. You've arrived in Lisbon, Portugal but when no one shows up to meet you, it's soon clear that you shouldn't be here. You have to head straight for 60.

86. You've tracked Kitty Litter to a small sugar beet farm. But when you ask around, no one here has seen her at all. Finally, you give up and go to 99.

87. The Rhine Maiden turns out to be an opera singer. The Rhine Maiden is also one of the heroines of the famous opera *The Ring of the Nibelung,* which was written by Richard Wagner. Although the singer is practicing when you arrive, she takes a break to talk with you. You ask her about the thief you're looking for.

"He was here," she tells you. "He had brown eyes and told me he was going to a place where he could find plenty of steel to steal."

You leave her to her practice and return to 156 to check out these leads.

88. You've arrived in Sofia, the capital of Bulgaria. As you get off the plane, you're met by a local police officer. He hands you a short list.

"The thief you're tracking was seen by these people," he explains. "And I've narrowed down the places she could have gone to just these three."

If you want to stay in Sofia and talk to:
Foma the farmer — go to 64
The shipworker — go to 101
Tereza the tomato picker — go to 169

If you're ready to move on to:
Lisbon, Portugal — go to 51
Paris, France — go to 92
Edinburgh, Scotland — go to 19

89. You've tracked Oly O'Leahy to Glasgow and find yourself at a soccer club. The team, the Glasgow Rangers, is playing at home, and there are thousands of people here. But not Oly isn't among them. Head for 99.

90. You reach Bucharest, Romania very early in the day, and there's no one to meet you. Though you wait several hours, nobody shows up. Finally, you head to 60.

91. Your plane touches down in Bucharest,

the capital of Romania. Two thousand years ago, Romania was a province of the Roman Empire, and even after it became an independent country, it still based its name on Rome. As you reach the information desk, one of the local officers comes over to greet you.

"I've found three people who saw your thief, and there are only three places he could have gone from here" he tells you, handing you a list. You thank him and look over your choices.

If you want to stay in Romania and question:
The gypsy violinist — go to 38
The pleasant peasant — go to 128
Sylvie from Transylvania — go to 71

If you're ready to move on to:
Sofia, Bulgaria — go to 104
Madrid, Spain— go to 160
Berlin Germany — go to 14

92. You're reached Paris, the capital of France. There isn't anyone here to meet you, though. When you call the local office, the agent on duty tells you to head straight to 60.

93. You arrive in Sofia, Bulgaria, but you're all alone. Head for 60.

94. The Hebrides are a group of islands off the northern coast of Scotland. Though there are about five hundred islands altogether, only about one hundred are inhabited. You find Heather living on Skye, one of the Inner Hebrides, and ask her about the thief you're trailing.

"He was here," she tells you. "He said he was looking for bauxite. When I told him that there wasn't any on the islands, he said he'd go where there was some."

You thank her and return to Kilmarnock (57) to check out this lead.

95. You've tracked Kitty Litter a long way to Tipperary, Ireland. When you finally arrive — you discover she isn't here. Time to head for 99.

96. You arrive in the Algarve, the beautiful southern coast of Portugal, looking for Lynn Gweeny. But though this is a very popular tourist spot, she isn't here. Finally, you have to give up and go to 99.

97. Your plane lands in Edinburgh, the capital of Scotland. When you get off, you discover that there's a message for you from the Chief. It reads: Go straight to 60.

98. Piraeus is the port for Athens, and when you arrive there, you find that the sailor you're looking for is about to leave on a merchant boat filled with olives. You've just got time to ask him about the man you're trailing.

"He took a ship out from here," the sailor tells you. "Brown-haired fellow. He said he was going to look for lead."

After thanking the sailor, you head back to Athens (74) to check out your clues.

99. Well, you've tracked the thief to the right place, but you've picked the wrong person as your suspect. That's not the way to become a world famous detective! It's time for you to head to the back of the book and check your score. But, because you tried to arrest the wrong person, add ten points to your travel points.

100. Although most of the tiny country of San Marino is dotted with farms, you have no trouble finding the farmer you're looking for. You ask him about the thief you're hunting.

"He went through here," the farmer tells you. "He was studying a book about learning to speak German. That's all I know."

You head back (79) to check out this clue.

101. Bulgaria borders on the Black Sea, which is 180,000 square miles in area. The country has a lively shipbuilding industry, and the man you're looking for is a worker in one of the shipyards. You find him and ask about the thief you're tracking.

"She came by here," he tells you. "She said she wanted a boat to go fishing, and I told her that we build boats for cargo, not for fishing. She left in a bad mood, saying she was going where she could find a lot of fishing boats."

You thank him for his help and head back to Sofia (88) to check this out.

102. You're out on the moors of Scotland, which can get very damp and foggy. You've managed to end up in thick mist, and you keep going around in circles. It doesn't matter much, though, because Kitty Litter isn't here anyway. When you get out of this fog, you'd better head for 99.

103. When you land in Sofia, Bulgaria, you discover that there isn't anyone here to meet you. Maybe it's an accident, but you don't think so. Sure enough, when you call the local Interpol office, you're told to head straight to 60.

104. You've reached Sofia, the capital of Bulgaria. But there isn't anyone here to greet you. Odd. Then you check with the local Acme office, and they tell you to report straight to 60.

105. You reach the town of Essen, in north-western Germany. It's part of the Ruhr industrial area, one of the biggest manufacturing areas in Europe. The man you're looking for works in one of the factories here, and when you find him, you ask him about the thief you're hunting.

"She came through here," he tells you. "She had bright hazel-colored eyes. And she mentioned that she was looking for bauxite. When I told her that we don't use it, she got all annoyed and said she'd go somewhere that does."

You head back to Berlin (39) to figure things out.

106. You find an old vine-covered house and knock at the door. When a nun answers, you ask for Madeline, who turns out to be a cheerful young girl with an active imagination. When you tell her that you're a detective, she laughs.

"Ah!" she smiles. "I knew that woman I saw was up to no good! The black-haired crook! I'm sorry I didn't capture her for you, but I did notice that she was reading a book about shipbuilding. She also mentioned something about changing her money to zlotys. I hope that helps you."

You thank Madeline and head back to your base (61) to check out this new information.

107. Varna is a large city near the Black Sea, and you find the farm just outside of town. Like many Bulgarian farms, this one grows wheat. The farmer is in one of the fields, cutting the wheat for market. When he sees you coming, he turns his combine harvester in your direction and shifts into top speed.

Quickly, you dive into a drainage ditch. It's just deep enough to protect you from the harvester, which passes harmlessly over you. Before the farmer can turn around to try again, you leap to your feet and jump onto the harvester from behind. You grab the farmer and throw him off the machine. Then you switch off the harvester and climb down.

"Right," you tell him, "spill the beans."

"I don't know anything!" he cries.

"You don't know not to mess with an Acme agent," you agree. "So you must be working with someone from Carmen's gang. Tell me about it."

He's too scared to talk, but you see him glance at his jacket, which is hanging over the driver's seat of the harvester. Quickly, you hand-cuff him and search the pockets of the jacket.

You've hit the jackpot! A list of names and addresses for all of Carmen's gang! Quickly, you look for the address of your suspect. If you think the thief is:

Oly O'Leahy — *go to 29*
Gene Yuss — *go to 70*
Kitty Litter — *go to 86*
Ken Hartley Reed — *go to 127*

Minnie Series — *go to 167*
Russ T. Hinge — *go to 143*
Gypsy Rose Lasagna — *go to 17*
Lynn Gweeny — *go to 45*

108. Your plane lands in Madrid, and you discover that there isn't anyone to meet you. You call the local Interpol office, and they tell you, "You should be at 60." You go there right away.

109. Greece grows lots of large olives, which are then sent all over the world. The Greeks take great pride in their olives, and the man you're after is inspecting a new batch when you find him. He's carefully grading the olives by size and by quality, and you wait until he's finished before you ask him about the woman you're looking for.

"She was here," he tells you. "She tried to steal a jar of my finest olives for a salad. I threw her out, of course. As she left, I saw she was reading a book about car manufacturing."

You thank him for his help and head back to 35 to check out this clue.

110. You've arrived in Copenhagen, the capital of Denmark. Denmark is actually made up of the Jutland Peninsula and about four hundred small islands — though only about one hundred of these are inhabited. Greenland and the Faroe Islands, in the North Atlantic Ocean, are also part of Denmark. You wonder how many of these islands you'll have to visit before you catch the thief you're after.

The local Interpol inspector has started the

work for you. She hands you a list.

"Three people saw the thief as she made her getaway. And I've figured out that she fled to one of these three cities." You compliment the agent on her work and look over the list.

If you want to stay in Denmark and speak to:
The bacon packer — go to 20
The porcelain painter — go to 146
Poul the palace guard — go to 65

If you've figured out that the thief
has gone to:
Tirana, Albania — go to 126
Belgrade, Yugoslavia — go to 154
Madrid, Spain — go to 48

111. Dalmatia is a strip of land in western Yugoslavia, along the Adriatic Sea. About three hundred little islands are scattered along the coast, and it's a very popular tourist area. It's also where the spotted dogs known as Dalmatians received their name.

The man you're looking for works as a boatman, ferrying people out to the many islands. You ask him about the thief you're chasing.

"I remember the man," the boatman replies. "He wanted to be ferried across to some little island, but he refused to pay me. So I refused to take him. Then he went away, angry."

"Any idea where he went?" you ask.

"Well, he was reading a book about the clothing industry."

You thank him for his help and return to Belgrade, Yugoslavia (131) to check out this clue.

112. You've tracked Gene Yuss to the town of Sligo, Ireland, but when you arrive the trail is completely cold. There's no sense in hanging about here — you'd better head straight for 99.

113. You're in sunny Madrid, but you have a funny feeling that something's not quite right. You find that there isn't anyone waiting for you, so you call the local Interpol office, only to be told that you've got to go to 60 right away.

114. The farmer in Albania is a poor man who works hard to feed his family and to grow crops to sell. He is very friendly, and you ask him about the crook you're tailing.

"She was here," he tells you. "She was looking for a good bottle of wine, so I told her she'd have to go somewhere else. She said she was going to do just that."

You thank him and head back to Tirana (52) to check out this lead.

115. Your plane touches down in Warsaw, the capital of Poland. But there's no sign of any contact here. After a short while, you ask at the information desk. The girl on duty smiles and hands you a new ticket. "This was left for you," she explains.

It's a ticket to 60. Better go there at once.

116. You've reached Dublin, the capital of Ireland — but you're here all alone. The local office hasn't sent anyone to meet you. Puzzled, you check in, only to be told to head straight for 60.

117. Donkey Jose turns out to be the owner of a small farm that breeds donkeys. They are used for riding and hauling in some parts of the country, and he's very proud of his sturdy little animals. You compliment him on his fine donkeys and ask about the woman you're after.

"She was here," he tells you, scowling. "Tried to steal one of my donkeys! I chased her off my farm fast enough! She even dropped her teach-yourself-German book when she went."

You leave him looking after his animals as you head back to Madrid (133) to check out this clue.

118. Poland produces a lot of coal, and it takes you a while to find the miner you're looking for. Finally, you see him as he's leaving work, still dusty and black from the mine. He stops to answer your questions.

"Yes, I saw the lady you're after," he says. "Gray eyes, she had, very pretty."

"Any idea where she went?" you ask.

"Well, she mentioned that she wanted to do some fishing," he tells you.

As he walks away, you head to Warsaw (16) to check out this clue.

119. There are a large number of banks in Switzerland. The bank manager you want to speak to agrees to see you between customers. After a few minutes, you ask about the thief you're tracking.

"Well, he was here," says the banker. "He wanted to open an account to store his stolen money. I told him that we don't do that sort of thing here, and he left in a very bad mood. Oh, and on the way out, he stopped to change his money into drachmas."

You thank him and do the same before you head back to Bern (1).

120. You're in Belgrade, Yugoslavia, but you start to wonder if you should be. You don't see your contact, so you call the local Acme office.

The secretary is surprised to hear from you and tells you that you're supposed to be at 60.

121. You've tracked Gene Yuss down to the River Tagus, one of the two largest rivers in Portugal. But this is where the trail stops. Since there isn't much else for you to do, you head off to 99.

122. The Scottish people are very proud of their arts and music, and you've arrived just in time for one of their festivals. The dancer you're looking for is doing a very difficult dance. He's dressed in traditional Scottish clothing — a kilt, which looks like a plaid skirt; and a sporran, a pouch that is worn in front of the kilt and that is used to hold things, since there aren't any pockets in a kilt. Two swords called claymores are placed on the ground in the shape of a cross. As the bagpipes play, the dancer has to step between the blades of the sword, being careful not to touch the swords with his feet. You can see it takes good concentration to do this dance!

As the man finishes, you go over to speak to him. When he sees you, however, he grabs one of the swords and charges at you, screaming at the top of his lungs.

One of Carmen's men, obviously! You dodge his

charge and grab the other sword — fast. You're just in time. He swings at you again, but you block him with the sword you're holding. You then grab his arm in a judo throw. With a twist, you send him flying.

"Now that's what I call a Highland Fling," you laugh.

The man is now unconscious. You search him quickly, and in his sporran you find a sheet of paper containing the names and addresses of all of Carmen's gang!

If you think the thief you're looking for is:

Gene Yuss — go to 4

Gypsy Rose Lasagna — go to 56

Russ T. Hinge — go to 162

Minnie Series — go to 77

Ken Hartley Reed — go to 40

Lynn Gweeny — go to 134
Kitty Litter — go to 102
Oly O'Leahy — go to 89

123. Ah, Paris! It seems so cheery and care-free here, with sidewalk cafes, women in bright fashions, and flowers everywhere. If only you had more time to stay and enjoy yourself. But, with a sigh, you drag your attention back to the case at hand. You decide to have a glass of Perrier water at one of the cafes while you wait for your contact to arrive .

Almost out of breath, the young girl from the local Acme office arrives. "Sorry I'm late," she apologizes, "but I've been checking out some hot tips." You order her a cold drink and wait for her to catch her breath. When her water arrives she takes a sip and hands you the list.

"I've located three people who saw your thief," she says. "And there are only three flights out of Paris that he could have taken before I had all the planes watched."

If you want to stay in Paris and speak to:
The boatman — go to 62
The artist — go to 5
The Louvre lover — go to 147

If you're ready to leave for:

Warsaw, Poland — go to 115
Bern, Switzerland — go to 1
Bucharest, Romania — go to 90

124. You've arrived in Wexford, Ireland famous all over the world for its beautiful crystal. It seems like a perfect spot to find Gypsy Rose Lasagna. She'd love to get her hands on some of the valuable glass. But no matter where you look, there isn't a sign of her. Finally you give up and head for 99.

125. So this is Vienna, the capital of Austria! All around the city are ancient palaces and grand homes from the time when this was the place to be in Europe. It was a time when orchestras would strike up the music, and partying couples would waltz, fox-trot, and polka the night away . It was a time when . . . You look at your watch. Goodness, the time! You hurry to meet your contact at the stately Kariskirche, the elegant church built in 1715. He waves to you cheerfully as you arrive.

"I've done some work," he tells you, handing you a slip of paper, "and I found a few people who saw your thief. I've checked, and there are only three places she might have gone to."

You compliment him on his work and review the list.

If you want to stay in Vienna and speak to:
The psychiatrist — go to 68
The cabinet maker — go to 15
The waiter — go to 84

If you're moving on to:
Warsaw, Poland — go to 145
Madrid, Spain — go to 113
Berlin, Germany — go to 39

126. You reach Tirana, in Albania. Albania is one of the poorest countries in Europe, and it's got another bad surprise for you — there's no one here to meet you. You'd better head for 60.

127. The town of Sofia, Bulgaria stands on the banks of the Iskur River. Your trail takes you up the river, about twenty-four miles to the huge Iskur Dam. This dam provides not only irrigation water for the farmers but also water to generate much of the electricity that runs Sofia. Here, at the dam, you spot Ken Hartley Reed.

Quietly, you sneak up on him and see that he's carrying the original copy of "Auld Lang Syne"! Excellent! Now all you have to do is arrest him . . .

He spins around and snarls as he sees you

coming. "I thought we'd stopped you, gumshoe."

"It'll take better men than you to stop me, Ken," you reply.

"Oh yeah?" he asks. Then he jumps at you.

You were expecting this. Twisting around, you karate chop his neck and then grab the song from him. He spins around to attack again, and this time you grab his arm and heave him right over your shoulder — into the water of the dam. As he thrashes in the water, you grab a life preserver and toss it to him. Then you drag him out of the water. You pull the life preserver down to below his shoulders, pinning his arms to his sides so he can't escape.

"Never mind, Ken," you say. Then you begin to sing "Auld Lang Syne" to him :

Should auld acquaintance be forgot
And never brought to min'?

"What?" he asks.

"You're one acquaintance I'd sure like to forget," you smile. "And, once you're safely in prison, I'll work on doing just that."

You call the police, who arrive to take Ken away. Then you phone the Chief to report your news, and you can tell he's really pleased with you. "Excellent work, detective!" he says. "Now head for the scoring chart at the back of the book and see if you've earned a promotion!"

128. Much of Romania is farmland. The peasant farmer you're looking for is out in the fields, working with his family. He greets you as you arrive, and you ask him about the thief you're tracking.

"He went by here," the farmer tells you. "He stopped to see what I grow, but when he found out that my crop is sugar beets, he carried on and on. He said he was looking for fruit."

You thank the peasant and head back to Bucharest (91) to check out this clue.

129. Like many European countries, Portugal has several native dances and musical styles. You arrive at a music hall, where a small band is playing. In the band is a guitarist, an accordian player, a drummer, and a violinist. Several dancers are demonstrating the fandango, the chula, and the verdegaio. You spot the dancer you're looking for and go over to meet him.

When he sees you, he snarls and heads straight for you. It's one of Carmen's men!

Thinking quickly, you pick up a guitar and smash it over the gunman's head. With a sigh, he collapses, an unconscious heap. A lucky escape! Better be on guard as you head back to Lisbon (51) to check out another contact.

130. Bialystok is a small town in Eastern Poland, quite close to the Soviet border. You discover that Max is a local theater manager. He's a rather fat man, with thinning hair, and he is wearing a silk robe over his clothes. "What do you want?" he asks when he sees you. "Are you a bill collector?"

"No," you tell him. "I'm a detective. I'm only here to ask you a few questions."

He leaps to his feet and smiles. "I'm good at questions," he promises. "I got an A on every paper I wrote in school."

You ask him about the thief you're trailing, and he nods, eager to please. "She was here, that robber! She said she was a bill collector and that I had to pay her the next six months' rent. The scoundrel! And she wanted me to pay her in pounds. Pounds! Can you believe it?"

"Yes," you tell him. "I can believe it. Probably getting ready to pull another move." You start to leave, but Max grabs your coat.

"Since you're not after me, how about selling me your trench coat — I just love American clothes!"

You free yourself from his grasp and rush downstairs. You can hear his voice following you: "All right! I'll pay you ten zlotys! Five? Five, and that's my last offer!"

You rush back to Warsaw (16) to note your

new clue — and to put as much space as you can between yourself and Max!

131. You've landed in Belgrade, the capital of Yugoslavia. The coastal area of Dalmatia is well known for its beautiful beaches and lovely islands. It's a shame you have to work, but catching Carmen's gang comes first.

Your local contact arrives and hands you a list. "I've identified three people who saw your thief," she tells you. "And three places he might have gone on to." You thank her and examine what she's found.

If you want to stay in Yugoslavia
and talk to:
The teacher — *go to 33*
A Dalmatian — *go to 111*
Sara from Sarajevo — *go to 139*

If you think the thief went to:
Vienna, Austria — *go to 21*
Lisbon, Portugal — *go to 78*
Sofia, Bulgaria — *go to 53*

132. After finding the town of Kinsale without much trouble, you start asking around for Keara. Finally, you track her down to the small cottage in which she lives and works. Keara is a weaver,

an expert with the loom. Many of Ireland's finest textiles are made in small cottages like hers.

When Keara sees you, though, she jumps to her feet and tries to attack you. You dodge her blows and whip out your handcuffs. Grabbing one of her wrists when she tries to hit you again, you slap on the cuffs and then fasten them to her heavy loom.

"That will keep you in place," you smile. "I gather you're working for Carmen Sandiego?"

"You'll get nothing out of me," she promises you. You can believe it, so you head back to Dublin (46) to try another lead. Better watch out for other surprises, though!

133. You've reached Madrid, the capital of Spain. The beautiful weather in Spain makes tourism a big industry here, so it takes some time going through the crowded streets to get to the information desk, where the local Interpol agent greets you. He's prepared a list for you to examine. The list shows the contacts the thief made and where she might have fled.

If you want to stay in Spain and investigate:
Dulcinea — go to 76
The Barber of Seville — go to 43
Donkey Jose — go to 117

If you're ready to travel to:
Bern, Switzerland — go to 11
Vienna, Austria — go to 125
Bucharest, Romania — go to 153

134. You arrive in the town of St. Andrews, Scotland, which has what many people consider to be the finest golf course in the world. You find Lynn Gweeny trying to get someone to play a game with her. Walking up softly behind her, you tap her on the shoulder.

"I don't think you'll have time for a game," you tell her. "Any minute now, the police will be here to arrest you. And they don't allow golfing in the local jails."

"I don't want to go to jail!" Lynn sobs.

"Then you shouldn't steal things," you reply. "Speaking of which, where's the Little Mermaid?"

"Back in my hotel bathtub ," she says. "I only took her because I thought the statue would look good in the middle of my pond back home."

"Well, don't worry about it," you tell her. "It'll look even better back where it belongs — in Copenhagen Harbor."

As the police take Lynn away, you call the Chief to tell him you've solved the case.

"Excellent," he answers. "I knew you'd crack the case. Why don't you head for the scoring chart at the back of the book to see if you've earned a promotion?"

135. You arrive in the town of Sozopol, on the shore of the Black Sea. You find the fisherman you're looking for loading his boat. When he sees you, though, he throws down his net and reaches for a high powered fishing rod lying on the floor of his boat. Ah-ha! One of Carmen's gang!

Thinking quickly, you snatch up one of the large fishing nets and throw it over him and pull it tight. He's dragged off his feet and hits his head on the deck.

You're safe, but he's out cold, so there'll be no information from him. You call the police to come down to the dock.

"You won't believe the catch of the day," you tell them. But you're still after the one that got away, so you head back to Sofia, Bulgaria (53) to try another lead. You'd better be on the look-out for trouble, though!

136. You arrive in Barcelona and soon find Carmen Over. She's a big fan of the bullfighters, which are called matadors in Spanish. You find her by the main bullring and ask her about the man you're after.

"He was here a little while ago," she replies.

"But he didn't stay to see the fight. He was in a hurry. I told him to slow down and have some fun, but he said he was going fishing."

"Yeah?" you nod. "And I'll bet what he's trying to catch is something valuable." You head back to Madrid (160) to check on this lead.

137. You enter the town of Elvas, in eastern Portugal, looking for Minnie Series. You ask around, and only one person remembers seeing her.

"She didn't stay long," he tells you. "She thought that this was Elvis. Big fan of rock and roll, I guess." Well, there's nothing more to be learned here. Better go to 99.

138. Montenegro is one of the six republics that divide Yugoslavia. You find Hugo, a musician, in the concert hall at Titograd. He's practicing with his small orchestra, playing themes from American cowboy movies. He stops the practice to talk to you, and you ask about the woman you're trailing.

"She was here," he tells you. "Didn't like my music much, I'm afraid. She said she was going somewhere to get fertilizer. I told her to stick her head in it and try to grow a little taste."

You leave him to his music and head back

to Belgrade, Yugoslavia (154) to check your information.

139. Sarajevo is one of the largest towns in Yugoslavia. You remember the name from school, because it was here, in 1914, that the assassination of Archduke Ferdinand became one of the causes of World War One. The town is peaceful now, and you find Sara fairly quickly. She's a language teacher, you learn. You ask about the man you're after.

"He stopped by here," she says. "He wanted me to help him learn Turkish. He was delighted that I could help — until he found out that he'd have to pay. Then he left in a hurry."

You hurry back to Belgrade, Yugoslavia (131).

140. You find that Matilde is a dance instructor with a studio near the Danube. She's a very cheery lady, who laughs when you ask about the man you're after.

"Such a strange person!" she exclaims. "He wanted me to teach him to waltz. And he wanted to pay me in stamps — said he collected them as a hobby. He was very offended when I refused, and he stomped down my stairs."

You thank her and rush back to home base (10).

141. Although Belgrade, Yugoslavia is a very nice city, you feel lost. There's no one here to meet you, so, after a while, you call the local Interpol office.

"What are you doing in Belgrade, Yugoslavia?" the receptionist asks you. "Don't you know you should be at 60?"

142. You've arrived in Edinburgh, the capital of Scotland. Scotland has been a part of the United Kingdom since King James VI of Scotland became James I of England in 1603. The two countries agreed to become Great Britain in 1707, and were later joined by Wales and Northern Ireland.

The local police chief arrives, looking a bit muddy. "Excuse the mess," he apologizes. "I was gardening in my yard when I heard about this case."

"Ah," you reply. "Scotland Yard!"

"Quite," he sighs. Obviously he's heard that one before. He hands you a short slip of paper. "Anyway, I've managed to —er— dig up three people for you to talk to." You check out his list.

If you want to investigate:

The Ghillie — go to 28

The soccer player — go to 158

The Highland dancer — go to 122

143. You've trailed Russ T. Hinge to Zlatograd, in southern Bulgaria. Though the area is warm, the trail is very, very cold. Finally, you have to give up in disgust and head for 99.

144. Peat moss, the compressed remains of marshes and trees, is generally found in swampy areas. In some parts of the world, peat moss is used as fuel. The man you're looking for is digging peat moss to sell in a muddy area of the hills. You go over to him and ask about the thief you're trailing.

Instead of answering you, though, he attacks you with his spade. After ducking the first swing, you get in a good punch. Startled, the peat man collapses backward into the mud.

Obviously, he's one of the gang! You must be getting close. Better head back to Dublin (46) to check on another lead — and keep your eyes open for more dirty deeds . . .

145. You've reached Warsaw, the capital of Poland. But when you get off the plane, there's nobody here to meet you. Puzzled, you call the local office, and you're told to report at once to 60.

146. Porcelain is a big seller in Denmark, and there are plenty of skilled craftspeople who paint plates, cups, and saucers for sale. The woman you are looking for is carefully painting patterns onto a dinnerplate when you arrive. You wait until she's finished, not wanting to ruin her concentration, and then ask her about the robber you're after.

"She was here," the artist tells you. "She tried to steal a plate from me. Luckily, I spotted her and threw her out."

"Any idea where she might have gone?" you ask.

"Well, I noticed that she was carrying a book about steelmaking."

After thanking the woman, you dash back to 110 to check out this clue.

147. The Louvre was originally a palace built during the reign of Louis XIV. It is now one of the most famous art museums in the world. On display in the Louvre are Leonardo da Vinci's

masterpiece, the *Mona Lisa*; James Whistler's *Arrangement In Gray and Black* (better known as *Whistler's Mother*); and the ancient Greek statue of Venus de Milo.

You wish you had the time to see the other treasures, but you must find the lady you're looking for. She comes here every day to admire the famous paintings and statues. When you ask about the man you're after, she nods her head.

"I saw him — what a wretch!" she cries. "He was looking for a way to steal the *Mona Lisa*. I was so furious I hit him with my umbrella!" She brandishes it like a sword. "Like this!" She smacks you too, until you calm her down.

"I can see he annoyed you," you tell her, thankful that she has stopped hitting you. "But do you have any idea where he went?"

"Well, I know he carried a book about potatoes."

You thank her and hurry back to 123 to check out this clue.

148. Bern, the capital of Switzerland, is a cold place high in the Alps. Figures, because your trail is ice-cold. There's nobody here to meet you. Time to head to 60, before you freeze.

149. You've trailed Russ T. Hinge to Montalegre, near the Portuguese border. But here you lose all track of him. After a while, you're forced to give up and head to 99.

150. You've arrived in Berlin, capital of Germany. There are a lot of people around, but not one of them is your contact. Puzzled, you call the office, only to be told to meet him at 60.

151. Sofia, Bulgaria is a very pretty city, and there are plenty of tourists in town. The man you're looking for is taking one group of them around the city. You find him at the church of St. George, parts of which date back to the third century. He's explaining all about the church when he spots you.

Suddenly, he rushes over to you, holding a huge guidebook over his head. You're sure he means to slam it over *your* head. But you haven't spent all that overtime learning defense methods for nothing. You pick up a large candlestick and use it to knock the book out of his hand. Then you punch him on the chin. Dazed, he's not able to resist the police who rush over to arrest him.

"You should stick to sites, not fights," you advise him. Then, watching your step, you head back to base (53) to check out more clues.

152. You've tracked Minnie Series to Cork, Ireland, but there you run into a dead end. There's no sign of her anywhere, so you have to give up and head to 99.

153. Bucharest, the capital of Romania, is a friendly city — but not for you. There's nobody here to welcome you. After a while, you head to the information desk at your hotel and ask if there are any messages. Indeed there is one, and it tells you to head straight to 60.

154. Belgrade, the capital of Yugoslavia, was founded in the third century by the native Celts. Belgrade is also known as the "fortress on water,"

because it is where the Danube and Sava rivers meet.

You spot your contact at the old fortress of Kalemegdan. He hands you a list of people to contact and possible places your thief may have gone.

If you want to stay in Yugoslavia
    and investigate:
The shoemaker from Zagreb — go to 12
Hugo from Montenegro — go to 138
The wine maker — go to 69

If you're ready to move on, for:
Athens, Greece — go to 170
Sofia, Bulgaria — go to 93
Tirana, Albania — go to 52

155. You're high in the Swiss Alps, near the famous Matterhorn. Here you find the yodeler you're searching for. Yodeling is a form of singing that is popular in Switzerland, but it's not something you like very much. You're glad when the yodeler stops singing and sits down to talk to you. You ask about the man you're hunting.

"He was here," the yodeler tells you. "A brown-eyed man. He mentioned that next he was going after oil."

You thank the man, and he starts back with his singing.

You're really glad to leave and get back to Bern (1) to check your information.

156. After World War II, Germany was split into two countries, East Germany and West Germany. Now, however, it is one nation again. You've arrived in Leipzig, and your Interpol contact greets you as you get off your plane.

"I've done some tracking," she tells you, handing you a slip of paper. "The man you're looking for met three people. And there are just a few places he might have gone to."

If you want to stay in Germany and speak to:
Hans from Hannover — go to 34
The German shepherd — go to 58
The Rhine Maiden — go to 87

If you've figured out that the thief
has gone to:
Vienna, Austria — go to 10
Bern, Switzerland — go to 164
Madrid, Spain — go to 108

157. Greece was the home of many famous philosophers, including Plato, Aristotle, and Socrates. These men taught young people over two thousand years ago, and the Greeks still look upon education as being very important. Your contact is a professor at the local university, and you ask him about the thief you're tracking.

"Yes, she came here," he tells you. "She was looking for information about lead mining."

You thank him for his help and head back to Athens (35) to check out this clue.

158. The Scottish take the game of soccer very seriously (although it's called football in Scotland!), and there are great rivalries between teams.

You arrive at the stadium where the local team is practicing and you see the man you're looking for is the left wing. You discover that this means that he plays on the left side of the field. As you go over to him, though, he suddenly rushes toward you and gets ready to start kicking you instead of the ball.

"Foul!" you yell and grab the ball. You throw it with all of your strength, and it hits him, knocking him off his feet. Before he can get up again, you slap handcuffs on him. "Penalty in my favor," you tell him. "You're off to jail!"

As soon as he's taken away by the local police, you head back to Edinburgh (142). That was a close one. You must be getting close to the thief!

159. Loch Ness is a small lake in northern Scotland, and if it weren't for the reports that a monster lives in it, Lock Ness probably wouldn't be famous. You glad that the monster is not what you're here to investigate.

You find the man you want near the quiet waters. You ask him about the thief you're after.

"You're *steal* on his trail?" the man jokes. You can see why he's called the Loch Ness Punster. "Well, the only thing he took here was the road out."

"Do you know where he went?" you ask.

"*Know*," he answers. "But he was trying to learn French."

You thank him and get back to Kilmarnock (57) fast, before the man drives you crazy with bad jokes.

160. You've reached Madrid, the capital of Spain. At 2,373 feet above sea level, Madrid is the highest capital city in Europe. This makes the air fresh and clear, and Madrid is a delightful city to visit. You're glad this isn't mid-summer, though, because then the heat can get really bad and make life miserable.

Making life happy for you is the local Interpol inspector, who arrives with a list for you to look over. "Those are the people who saw your thief," he tells you. "And the possible places he may have gone to when things got too hot for him here."

If you want to stay in Spain and talk to:
The orange picker — go to 67
Carmen Over — go to 136
The fruit inspector — go to 6

If you're ready to go on to: 👈

Belgrade, Yugoslavia — go to 120
Copenhagen, Denmark — go to 83
Dublin, Ireland — go to 46

161. You've reached the banks of the Zezere River in central Portugal. The person you're looking for is perched on an old bridge, fishing quietly. When he sees you coming, though, he pulls his rod back and then casts his hook at you. He's trying to tie you up in his fishing line! Obviously, he's working for Carmen and her gang!

As you manage to duck the hook, you slip the hook onto the bridge railing. "Catch this!" you tell him, and he pulls hard. With a cry, he topples into the river. When he struggles up to the bank, you're waiting, and you use his own fishing line to tie him up.

The police arrive to take him away, and you head back to Lisbon (51) to follow another clue. You'd better be on the look-out for more trouble, though. You must be getting close to the big fish you're after!

162. You're in Inverness, on Ben Nevis, which, at 4,400 feet, is the tallest mountain in the British Isles. You've tracked Russ T. Hinge this far, but now there's no sign of him. For all you can know, he might have fallen off the moun-

tain. Since there's nothing else you can do, you head to 99.

163. Zoe and Chloe turn out to be twins who live in Litokhoron, a small town on the slopes of Mount Olympus, Greece. Olympus was where the Greek Gods of Mythology were supposed to have lived. It's a tall mountain, almost ten thou-

sand feet high, and very impressive. You can see why everyone thought that Gods lived there.

You ask the girls about the man you're after, and they giggle.

"He wanted to double date us," they say together. "But we told him to clear off."

"Any idea where he went?" you ask them. "None at all," they tell you, giggling again.

You realize that they are going to be no help at all, so you head back to Athens (74) and hope for better luck with your next lead.

164. You've reached Bern, the capital of Switzerland. But there isn't anyone here to meet you. Puzzled, you call the local Interpol office.

What are you doing here?" the local agent asks. "You're supposed to have gone to 60."

165. You've tracked Gypsy Rose Lasagna to a small cafe in Lisbon. But when you arrive, you discover the cafe has been out of business for several months. Not only has the food gone cold, but so has the trail. Sighing, you head for 99.

166. You reach Vlora and find the factory you're seeking. The man you want to speak to works here, and you find him just as he's about

to go home for the day. When you ask about the crook you're trailing, he thinks hard.

"Yes, I saw her," he remembers. "She wanted to know where she could change her money into francs."

Thanking him, you head back to Tirana, Albania (52) to follow up on this lead.

167. You've tracked Minnie Series to Plovdiv, a large town in central Bulgaria. But here the trail stops. She's disappeared completely, so you pack up and head for 99.

168. You've arrived in Dingle, the town on Dingle Bay where Lynn Gweeny is supposed to be hiding. But nobody has seen her, and you realize that you've followed a false clue. With a sigh, you head for 99.

169. Tomatoes are a big crop in Bulgaria, and Tereza is a worker in one of the farms that grows them. When you arrive, you find her picking tomatoes carefully from the vines. You ask her about the woman you're tracking.

"I saw her," Tereza recalls. "She was passing through here. She mentioned that she was on her way to a place she could get a few bottles of very good wine."

You return to Sofia, Bulgaria (88) to check out this clue.

170. You've reached Athens, the capital of Greece. Once a center of international learning, you learn one thing: this isn't the right place to be. You'd better head for 60.

SCORING CHART

Add up all of your travel points (you did remember to mark one point for each time you moved to a new number, didn't you?) If you have penalty points for trying to arrest the wrong person, add those in too. Then check your score against the chart below to see how you did.

0 – 17: You couldn't really have solved these cases in these few steps. Either you're boasting about your abilities or you're actually working with Carmen's gang. Be honest and try again — if you dare!

18 – 40: Super sleuth! You work very well and don't waste time. Well done — you deserve the new rank and the nice, big bonus you'll get next payday!

41 – 60: Private eye material! You're a good, steady worker, and you get your man (or woman). Still, there's room for improvement, and you can always try again to get another promotion.

61 – 80: Detective first class. You're not a world-famous private eye yet, but you're getting there. Try again and see if you can move up a grade or two!

81 – 100: Rookie material. You're taking too long to track down the crooks. Next time, they're going to get away from you. Try a little harder and see if you're really better than this.

Over 100: Are you sure you're really cut out to be a detective? Maybe you'd be better off looking for an easier job — a janitor for Acme , maybe? Still, if you're determined to be a detective, why not try again and see if this was just an off day. Better luck next time!